Soccer 'Cats Team Roster

Lou Barnes	*Striker*
Jerry Dinh	*Striker*
Stookie Norris	*Striker*
Dewey London	*Halfback*
Bundy Neel	*Halfback*
Amanda Caler	*Halfback*
Brant Davis	*Fullback*
Lisa Gaddy	*Fullback*
Ted Gaddy	*Fullback*
Alan Minter	*Fullback*
Bucky Pinter	*Goalie*

Subs:

Jason Shearer

Dale Tuget

Roy Boswick

Edith "Eddie" Sweeny

Chapter 1

It was a beautiful sunny day, just perfect for soccer. Lou Barnes couldn't wait to get to the field. The Soccer 'Cats were taking on the Panthers today. The Panthers were always a tough team, but Lou had a feeling that the 'Cats were going to come out on top.

He rummaged around in his room, looking for his lucky soccer ball. He'd scored his first goal with that ball. Coach Bradley had let him keep it after the game, and now Lou brought it with him whenever the 'Cats played. He finally found it buried in his closet. He tucked

the ball under his arm and headed down-stairs.

Lou knew that some people looked strangely at the arm holding the ball. True, that arm wasn't quite the same as his other arm. It was a little shorter, and couldn't move the same way his other arm moved because it was partly paralyzed.

He'd been born that way, so he never knew what it was like to have two arms that were the same. Things that most people used two arms and hands for—like playing a game of catch or using a fork and knife—he'd had to learn to do with one. His parents had hired a woman to help him learn, and over time he'd figured out his own way of doing things.

Sometimes, though, he caught someone he didn't know staring at him. At a country fair one time, a few older kids made fun of him. Lou had been so upset he'd almost started to cry. But for the most part, people treated him like any other kid—which was just fine with

Lou. That's how he thought of himself, after all.

All that was far from Lou's mind this morning, though. Now all he could think about was getting to the field and facing the Panthers! He waved good-bye to his mother, who was out back working in the garden, then jogged off to the game.

The field was crowded with Panthers and 'Cats. They did some warm-up drills, then got into position for the game. The 'Cats had won the coin toss. The referee placed the ball in the center circle, then backed away. Stookie, the 'Cats' center striker, stood next to the ball, waiting for the whistle. When it came, he toed the ball to Jerry Dinh on his left.

Jerry controlled it and took off. He dribbled past one defender. Then two Panthers double-teamed him. Coach Bradley had taught his team that when two defenders were guarding you, it meant that one of your teammates was wide open. Lou could see Jerry looking frantically for that open player. Finally, he saw Dewey London waving. He kicked the ball as hard as he could to him.

Dewey ran to meet the ball. He reached it just before the Panthers' center got to it. Dewey dribbled on an angle toward Lou's side of the field.

Lou knew that if he could get open, Dewey would pass it to him. He tried to break free of the Panther near him, but she stuck to Lou like glue. Dewey ended up passing the ball to Stookie.

Chapter 2

Rats!" grumbled Lou as he watched Stookie race downfield. Lou ran parallel to him, hoping to help out. His defender matched him step for step. There was no way Stookie would pass to him when she was so close, Lou thought.

He was right. When the Panther defense rushed Stookie, Stookie glanced at Lou, frowned, then passed the ball to Jerry. Jerry stopped it, dribbled a few paces closer to the goal, then shot the ball back to Stookie. Stookie wound up and took a mighty shot on goal. It all happened so fast that the Panthers' goalie didn't have a chance. The ball bounced into the net for the 'Cats' first score of the game.

The 'Cats cheered and jumped for joy, then hurried back to their starting positions. Lou was happy they were ahead. He hoped he'd have a chance to give the 'Cats an even bigger lead.

But he didn't. The whole first half, the Panther covered him like a blanket. He tried dodging around her, stopping short then speeding up, and weaving from side to side. Nothing worked.

Finally, a few minutes before the end of the half, he decided to try something a little more daring. He was going to run full out for the Panthers' goal.

He waited for Stookie to get the ball and start dribbling downfield. Then he took off. Legs pumping, he ran for all he was worth and managed to leave his defender several

steps behind! Keeping one eye on Stookie, he made a beeline for the goal.

Phreet!

Lou stopped short at the whistle. He looked around to see what had made the ref stop the game. To his horror, he saw the ref pointing straight at him.

"Offside!" the ref shouted.

Lou slapped his hand to his head. He'd forgotten a basic soccer rule: If you don't have the ball and you're in your opponent's half of the field, you have to keep at least two defenders between you and the goal. Otherwise, you're offside.

The only defender between Lou and the goal was the goalie. Lou had run so fast, he'd outrun the Panthers' fullbacks as well as the girl defending him.

The ref positioned the ball for an indirect free kick. A Panther fullback took the kick and sent it rocketing down the field. The girl who had been dogging Lou all game trapped it, spun, and headed for the 'Cats' goal. She dodged past the defense, and suddenly it was just her against the 'Cats' goalie.

"C'mon, Bucky, stop her!" Lou pleaded. But the Panther's kick was just too strong. Bucky lunged and missed. The score was tied — and it was all Lou's fault.

Chapter 3

Lou felt awful as he got back into position. He eyed the Panther across from him. She smiled triumphantly back at him.

If I'm going to make up for that mistake, Lou thought, *I've got to figure out a way to beat her!*

As the minutes ticked by, Lou tried every trick he knew. He speeded up, then stopped short. He faked left and moved right. He even stood stock-still, hoping she'd run past him. But nothing worked. He just couldn't shake her.

Finally, though, something happened that

changed his luck. Midway through the second half, the Panther was taken out of the game and a sub was put in her place.

All right! Lou thought. *Now maybe I'll get a chance to help out in this game. Maybe I'll even make a goal!*

And it seemed like he was going to get a chance to do just that. With three minutes left in the game, Stookie was racing down the field with the ball. He glanced up at Lou, then jerked his head.

Lou was sure Stookie was signaling for him to head for the goal for a pass. He took off.

Lou was so focused on Stookie, he didn't think to check out the field in front of him. He saw Stookie stop and control the ball. Lou moved a few steps closer to the goal as Stookie pulled his leg back for the pass.

The pass was perfect. Lou had no trouble controlling the ball. *There's no way I'm missing this one!* Lou thought gleefully. He aimed and kicked. Suddenly, a blur of movement caught his eye. He heard a growl, and one second later, he was pulled to the ground!

Lou hit the turf hard. As he lay there, he heard the ref's whistle. Then he heard laughter.

Stookie appeared at Lou's side and helped him up. "What happened?" Lou asked, dazed.

"A dog knocked you down and ruined your shot," Stookie replied.

"What?!" Lou couldn't believe his ears.

"Afraid so," Stookie said. He looked like he didn't know whether to laugh or be angry.

"But the ball was going in! There was no way I was going to miss that shot! The ref has to count the goal, right?"

Stookie shrugged. "I don't think so. Besides, I think you were offside when I passed to you."

Lou's jaw dropped. He ran off the field to ask Coach Bradley. But the coach confirmed what Stookie said. The ball hadn't gone into the net, so it wasn't a goal.

Lou was furious. "But—but—" he sputtered

helplessly. Coach Bradley patted Lou's shoulder and shook his head.

The ref had finally managed to shoo the dog off the field. A fan held on to him while the game played out its last minute. When the buzzer sounded, the game ended in a tie.

"We should have won that game," Lou fumed to Roy. "It's all that stupid mutt's fault." The fan had let the dog go, and he was running around the field again. Lou turned in disgust, picked up his lucky soccer ball, and started for home.

Chapter 4

Lou hadn't gone more than two blocks when he heard a bark. Looking over his shoulder, he saw the dog running toward him. A moment later, he was by Lou's side.

"What do you want?" Lou yelled, stopping. "Get out of here!"

The dog sat down and looked up at him. His eyes were soft brown. One pointy ear stood straight up, while the other one flopped to one side. His mouth was open, and it looked like he was laughing.

"Didn't you hear me, mutt? I said, get out of here!"

The dog gave a bark, then jumped up and knocked the soccer ball out from under Lou's arm. The ball landed on a crack in the sidewalk and bounced sideways into the street.

"Hey!" Lou glared at the dog and started to step off the sidewalk.

All at once, the dog lunged at him. He caught hold of Lou's soccer shirt and began to pull.

"What are you—" Lou started to shout. Just then, a huge truck barreled by them, blaring its horn. When the truck had passed, the dog let go of Lou's shirt.

The wind from the truck had blown Lou's hair into his face. Heart hammering in his chest, Lou brushed it back. He stared at the dog.

"You—you just saved my life, didn't you?" he said shakily, kneeling down next to the dog. The dog licked his face.

When his heart had slowed back to normal, Lou stood up and retrieved his ball. With a glance at the dog, he started walking back home again. The dog stayed at his side the whole way.

When they reached the house, Lou put his soccer ball on the front step and sat down. "Are you a stray?" he wondered. The dog had no collar, but he looked too well fed to be a stray. And weren't strays supposed to be mean?

"Well, if you're not a stray, then where'd you come from?" Lou asked. The dog didn't answer, of course. Instead, he nosed the soccer ball closer to Lou and gave a short bark.

"You want to play?" Lou said, grinning. "Okay!"

He opened the gate to their big backyard. The dog rushed through, barking happily, and ran to the far side of the yard. He seemed to be waiting for something. With a shrug, Lou gave the soccer ball a kick toward him.

The dog jumped in front of it, trapping it with his paws. Then he quickly nosed it back to Lou before hurrying back to the other end of the yard.

Lou was astonished. "Hey, where'd you learn to dribble like that?" He kicked the ball a second time. Again, the dog lunged for it. This time, he batted the ball around with his paws a little longer before bringing it back to Lou.

"I don't believe it," Lou said, shaking his head. "Let's see what else you can do!" He kicked the ball up in the air.

The ball arced toward the dog. The dog watched it carefully. As it started to drop, he ran underneath it.

"Watch out!" Lou cried.

Chapter 5

But Lou needn't have worried. Moments before the ball hit him, the dog jumped up, caught the ball on his head, and sent it rocketing back toward Lou. It came so fast, Lou couldn't catch it.

"A perfect header!" Lou shouted as he ran to retrieve it. The dog chased him. "Oh, no you don't!" Lou said, picking up speed. "I'm going to get it first!"

Lou did get to the ball first, but the dog was close behind. Lou fell on the ball, and the dog fell on Lou. They tussled for a moment. Then the dog started licking Lou's face. Lou collapsed in giggles and finally let go of the ball.

"You won't hurt my ball, will you?" he cried as the dog pawed it, growling. "It's lucky!"

The dog looked up suddenly and gave a bark.

"What is it, boy?" Lou asked. "Is it something I said? Was it the word 'lucky'?" The dog barked again. Lou slapped his hand to his head. "It *was* lucky! I bet your name is Lucky, isn't it?!"

"Who are you talking to?" a voice behind him asked.

Lou turned to see his mother standing in the doorway.

Lou moved so his mother could see the dog. "This mutt." He was about to tell her how the dog had saved his life. But at the last second, he changed his mind. Sometimes his mother worried about him, because of his arm. Lou didn't want her to think there was anything to worry about.

"Er, this mutt followed me home," he said instead. "I think his name is Lucky." The dog looked up at Mrs. Barnes, his tongue lolling out the side of his mouth.

Mrs. Barnes laughed. "He's adorable," she said. "And I bet he's thirsty, too. I'll get him some water."

Lou was surprised. They didn't have a pet. Lou had asked for a dog once, when he was five, but his parents had said it wasn't a good time for them to get a pet. Lou hadn't brought it up again, and his parents had never offered to get him one. He'd just figured they didn't like animals that much. But maybe he was wrong.

His mother returned a moment later, carrying a pan of water. Lucky drank, sloshing some onto the grass. Mrs. Barnes sat down next to Lou.

"No collar, huh?" she observed. Lou shook his head. She put an arm around his shoulders. "You know we can't keep him, don't you?"

Lou looked at his shoes. "Yeah, I know. Because you and Dad don't want to have pets, right?"

Mrs. Barnes's eyes widened. "Whatever gave you that idea?" she said. "We can't keep him because he obviously belongs to someone else. That person is probably worried sick." She reached out and patted Lucky's back. "Wouldn't you be?"

Lou knew she was right. Still, it made his throat tighten up knowing he might never see Lucky again. He'd only known him a short while, but already he knew he loved him.

Lou stroked Lucky's back. Lucky looked up at him, his muzzle dripping with water. Lou laughed and hugged him.

"I wish you were my dog," he whispered into Lucky's fur. Lucky rumbled deep in his chest.

Chapter 6

The next day, Lou and his mother walked downtown to put up some posters they'd made the day before. The posters showed Lucky's picture with the word "Found" above it. Underneath was the Barnes's phone number. Every time a shopkeeper let them tape one up, Lou's heart sank. If no one could see the posters, then Lucky's real owner might not be able to find him.

Lou and Lucky had had a wonderful afternoon the day before. They'd played some more soccer while his mother took some

photos of Lucky. When his mother went to have the photos developed, Lou found a rope and took Lucky for a walk.

Mrs. Barnes was carrying a big bag of dog food when she came home. "He'll have to spend the night with us, of course," she said.

While Mrs. Barnes was fixing dinner, Lucky chowed down a huge bowl of food and drank some more water. Then he padded to the door and looked over his shoulder.

"Well, at least he knows not to do his business inside the house!" Mrs. Barnes said, smiling. Lou took Lucky outside, where they played catch with a stick until dinner.

When Mr. Barnes came home, they all sat down to eat. He hadn't seen Lucky yet. But he felt him soon enough. Lucky plopped down right on top of his feet!

Mr. Barnes gave a yelp. "What is that?" he cried, looking under the table.

Mrs. Barnes laughed. "Howard, meet Lucky."

Lou held his breath. Would his father like Lucky as much as his mother did?

Mr. Barnes blinked. Then he smiled. "Well, hello there, fella," he said softly. He gave Mrs. Barnes a look. "Is he ours?"

Lou knew what the answer was, but he was still disappointed when his mother replied, "Only until we find his real owner."

But that had been the only bad part of the night. After dinner the whole family had taken Lucky for a walk. Then Lou and his dad made a bed out of a cardboard box and some old blankets. Mr. Barnes hesitated for only a moment before putting the bed in Lou's room.

The last thing Lou saw that night before he turned off the light was Lucky looking up at him. A warm feeling had spread throughout Lou.

That warm feeling was gone now, though. Now all he could feel was loneliness at the thought of Lucky going home with his real owner.

Chapter 7

The next two days, each time the phone rang, Lou's heart jumped into his throat. But no one ever called to claim Lucky. Lou continued to take care of him and play soccer with him. He even brought him to a soccer practice.

"Hey," said Roy Boswick, coming up to Lou, "isn't that the same dog that blocked your goal the other day?"

Lou nodded and explained. Roy whistled.

"Boy, too bad 'finders keepers' doesn't

work with animals," he said. "That dog sure looks like fun." He scratched Lucky behind the ears before joining the rest of the 'Cats.

Lou led Lucky to the bleachers. He'd bought him a collar and a leash the day before. Now he looped the leash around a pole. Lucky whined.

"Sorry, boy," Lou said, giving the dog a pat. "But this practice is for kids only." With one last glance over his shoulder, he ran to where the coach was outlining the first drill.

"This drill will help your reflexes and make you think about whether you're offside or not," Coach Bradley was saying. "Three lines, each line has a ball. Two offensive players dribble as fast as they can toward one defender and a goalie. When I blow the whistle, stop short. The player with the ball passes it to his partner. Then the partner dribbles fast again until the next whistle. The player without the ball must keep up with his partner but be sure to stay onside. Keep going all the way down the field. When you get to the end, make a goal if you can."

The kids formed the lines, and the coach doled out the balls. Then he blew the whistle, and the drill started. For several minutes, the only sounds were the coach's whistle blasting and the heavy breathing of the players who'd just finished their turns — and Lucky barking now and then.

Lou was in the line closest to the bleachers. He could see Lucky straining on his leash.

I wonder how strong that leash is? Lou thought as he and Bundy Neel took off for their turn.

He found out a moment later. The coach had just blown the whistle, and Lou had jammed to a stop. He was waiting for Bundy's pass when suddenly he was attacked by a bouncing ball of fur! Lucky had broken free and was tugging Lou's shirt!

"Down, Lucky, no!" Lou cried, trying to shake the dog off. Lucky finally stopped.

"What was that all about?" Lou asked, perplexed.

"I think I know!" replied Eddie Sweeny. She had been playing defense against Lou and Bundy's attack. "I know it sounds impossible, but I think Lucky was trying to pull you back onside!"

"No way!"

Eddie shook her red hair. "All I know is, you were offside a second ago until Lucky pulled you back onside."

The coach started laughing. "I'm afraid she's right, Lou—about you being offside, at least. I was about to blow my whistle when Lucky interrupted."

"I bet that's what he was doing in the game the other day!" Lou cried.

"Oh, great," groaned Jason Shearer. "That dog knows the rules of soccer better than the 'Cats!"

Chapter 8

No one could remember when they'd had more fun at a practice. With Lucky watching like a hawk from the sidelines, Lou and the others were much more careful about staying onside. At the end of practice, Lou even showed how Lucky could head the ball.

"He heads better than you do, Amanda!" Eddie said with a grin.

The 'Cats all headed for home tired but happy. No one was as happy as Lou, though. Everyone had treated Lucky as if he were Lou's dog. He'd liked that a lot.

Lou was whistling as he turned the corner onto his street. Then he stopped short. There was a car in his driveway. He'd never seen it before, but he knew right away who it belonged to: Lucky's real owner.

Lou wanted to run back to the field. Instead, he crossed the street and went into his house.

"Lou? Is that you?" his mother called from the kitchen. Lou hesitated, but Lucky didn't. He barreled down the hall and right to his water dish on the kitchen floor. Lou followed much more slowly.

Seated at the kitchen table were two men, one young and one old. The old one gave Lou a gentle smile.

"Hello, Lou," he said. He pointed to the young man. "That's Roger, and I'm Ben Wakefield." He held out his hand for Lou to shake.

Lou hated shaking hands. It wasn't that he didn't want to be friendly. But people always

held out their right hands. Lou's right hand was the paralyzed one. It was hard for him to shake hands with it. But if he held out his left hand instead, people always looked confused and embarrassed.

He was trying to decide what to do when, with a start, he saw that Mr. Wakefield was sitting in a wheelchair. Lou blinked. He knew how he liked to be treated when people saw he was a little different. He figured Mr. Wakefield would want to be treated that way, too. So Lou lifted his paralyzed arm and put his hand into Mr. Wakefield's with a warm smile. Mr. Wakefield's smile widened.

"Woof!"

Lou jumped. For a moment, he'd forgotten all about Lucky. Now he couldn't help but remember why Mr. Wakefield was there.

"Come here, boy," Mr. Wakefield called softly. Lucky padded over and put his head in Mr. Wakefield's lap. Mr. Wakefield stroked Lucky's head.

"You've taken fine care of him, Lou," he said. "I hope I'll be able to do the same."

Lou was confused. "What do you mean?" he asked. "Weren't you the one taking care of him before me?"

Mr. Wakefield shook his head. "Lucky is my son Jeff's dog," he said. "But Jeff was just transferred overseas. So Lucky's come to live with me until Jeff returns home in a few months."

"Oh," said Lou. He felt as if his whole world had just collapsed.

Chapter 9

Mr. Wakefield explained how he'd lost Lucky the week before.

"I'd taken him to the park next to the soccer field so he could run around," he said. "He's usually very good about staying close by. But Jeff had taught him how to play soccer, and now whenever Lucky is near a soccer game he just wants to join in. I'd forgotten about that until it was too late. By the time I'd wheeled myself around the park, the game was over and Lucky was nowhere in sight."

Lou told Mr. Wakefield how Lucky had followed him home and saved him from the truck. Mrs. Barnes raised her eyebrows when she heard that, but she didn't say anything.

Too soon, it was time for Mr. Wakefield to leave. Roger wheeled him out the door and helped him into his car. Lucky sat in the back, his head hanging out the window. Lou tried not to cry as the car backed out and pulled away. He heard Lucky give a bark—and then the car was gone.

Mrs. Barnes hugged him tight. "I know you're sad now," she said. "But your dad and I have agreed that if you want to get your own dog, you can. You've proven you're ready to take care of one."

But Lou shook his head. "Thanks anyway, Mom," he mumbled. "But the only dog I want is Lucky." Choking back tears, he ran inside and up to his room.

He flung himself onto his bed and cried. He wanted to hate Mr. Wakefield for taking Lucky away, but he couldn't. Lucky belonged

to Mr. Wakefield. There was nothing Lou could do about it.

The next morning Lou's head hurt. The last thing he wanted to do was play soccer. Everybody would ask him why he hadn't brought Lucky with him. He wasn't sure he'd be able to tell them without crying.

But his mother gently encouraged him to put his uniform on and go. "It'll be a lot better than moping around the house all day," she said. "And your friends will understand, Lou." So in the end, he'd tucked his lucky soccer ball under his arm and trudged off to the field.

The game against the Tadpoles started out rocky. Lou messed up an easy play that should have resulted in a goal. That made Stookie mad. He started yelling at everyone. When Bundy yelled at Stookie to stop yelling at everyone, Stookie got even madder. He took his anger out on the soccer ball, kicking it so hard that it was impossible for anyone to control. And that just made him madder still.

Finally, Coach Bradley subbed Roy in for Stookie. Stookie looked shocked, but knew better than to argue with the coach.

One look at Stookie on the beach reminded Lou that he, too, could wind up there if he didn't start paying attention.

Better start thinking about the game, he scolded himself, *instead of some stupid old dog who probably doesn't even remember who you are.*

Chapter 10

Roy did his best at Stookie's position, but he just wasn't as good a player as Stookie. He missed a couple of easy shots and was beaten by the Tadpoles' offense whenever he tried to help out on defense. Lou tried to do his part, but his heart wasn't really into it. That left Jerry as the sole offensive force—but he couldn't win the game alone. When the ref blew his whistle signaling halftime, the score was Tadpoles 2, 'Cats 1.

Stookie was red with frustration. He opened

his mouth to shout at them, but a hand on his shoulder from the coach closed it again.

"You 'Cats seem a little out of it today," Coach Bradley observed. "What will it take for you to start playing better?"

"Luck!" shouted Jason Shearer.

The coach groaned. "Very funny. I was thinking more along the lines of concentration. Pay attention to where the ball is, where you are, and where the Tadpoles are. I don't expect you all to play like superstars, but I do hope you'll at least focus on the game." He shot Lou a quick glance.

Lou kicked his toe in the dirt. A pebble bounced off his sneaker and ricocheted into his lucky soccer ball. The ball wobbled, then started to roll down the hill.

Lou moved to go after it. Then he stopped short, unable to believe what he was seeing. There was Lucky, nosing his ball back up the hill! Lou rushed to the dog and flung his arms around him.

The Soccer 'Cats crowded around them, cheering and laughing. Lou tried to look over them to see if Mr. Wakefield was there.

Finally, he spotted him. Roger was pushing him up the paved walkway that led to the field. Lou broke free of the 'Cats and led Lucky over to the pair.

Roger was breathing hard and sweating. He excused himself to get a drink from the 'Cats' watercooler. Mr. Wakefield looked at Lou with a twinkle in his eye.

"Roger's been chasing after that dog all morning," he whispered. "I think he's a little tired!"

Lou tried to hand Lucky's leash to Mr. Wakefield. But Mr. Wakefield waved it away.

"That doesn't belong to me," he said, looking straight into Lou's eyes.

Lou's heart pounded. Was Mr. Wakefield talking about the leash — or — or Lucky?

Mr. Wakefield took hold of Lou's righ

hand. He gave it a squeeze and said, "You heard me right. Lucky is yours."

"Why—? How—?" Lou couldn't seem to get his tongue to work.

"Roger's tried his best to keep up with Lucky, but it's hard when he's got to care for me, too. So I talked with Jeff last night," Mr. Wakefield explained. "Jeff agreed with me that Lucky would be much better off with an active young boy than an old man. There's just one condition."

"What's that?" Lou asked anxiously. What if he couldn't do it?

Mr. Wakefield laughed. "You have to play soccer with him every day. Think you can do that?"

Lou laughed and swept an arm toward the other 'Cats. "I think I—I mean we—can probably handle that!"

SOCCER 'CATS